Dear, Lili
Merry x-mas!
Love,
Lu

Sweet
Dreams ◡

Published by Grandreams Books Ltd,
4 North Parade, Bath, BA1 1LF, UK.

Grandreams Books Inc.,
360 Hurst Street, Linden, NJ 07036 USA
Printed in China.

50 BEDTIME STORIES

Written by Ann McKie.
Illustrated by Ken McKie.

CONTENTS

The Wee Island Of Loch Noddie

Little Red Mac and his friend Tam O'Tatie walked down by the shores of Loch Noddie.

"I've heard it said," Tam O'Tatie spoke very seriously, "that music can bring the Monster out of the Loch!"

So Tam O'Tatie took out his bagpipes and began to play.

And while he marched too and fro playing fit to burst, his friend Little Red Mac kept a sharp look out across the lake, just in case the Monster appeared.

"Piping makes me feel hungry!" said Tam O'Tatie, pausing for breath.

"Then let's find a place for a picnic." said Little Red Mac, (as he always carried a basket full of food wherever he went).

So they waded out to a tiny island which neither of them had ever noticed before.

"This must be a new island." said Little Red Mac as he climbed up the side and got on the top.

"I know a tune called 'The Wee Island Of Loch Noddie'" said Tam O'Tatie after they had eaten their picnic. "I shall play it for you on the bagpipes!"

No sooner had Tam O'Tatie started to play, than the new island slowly sank into the water, and an awful groaning noise came from the loch.

"It must be the Monster!" yelled Little Red Mac as he made for the shore.

"You silly man!" Tam O'Tatie said. "It's my bagpipes!"............now what do you think it was?

Congratulations, Mr Tappit!

"Tomorrow," said Mr Tappit the toy-maker, I shall have been making toys for fifty years!" and he locked up his toyshop and went home for tea.

All the toys in the shop overheard what Mr Tappit had said.

"We'll have a party tomorrow." said the baby doll.

"With presents!" said Teddy.

"And fireworks!" cried a shelf full of toys.

"We could have all three!" shouted the wind-up toys. "A party, presents and fireworks!"

"Don't forget a great big cake!" squeaked the tiny clockwork mouse.

"Let's get busy at once." said Teddy, and the toys gathered round.

By next morning, everything was ready.

Mr Tappit unlocked his toyshop as usual and stepped inside.......and there in the middle of the floor, was the biggest cake he had ever seen.

All of a sudden there was a pop and a loud bang, and toys of all shapes and sizes jumped out of the gigantic cake.

Some of them had presents, some of them had cards, and one of them was holding a beautiful iced cake.

"Congratulations, Mr Tappit!" all the toys cried as they waved flags and threw streamers.

"What a surprise." laughed Mr Tappit quite out of breath. "You've made me very happy!"

"We're having fireworks tonight!" squeaked the tiny clockwork mouse as he scampered off to eat his cake.

Silver Lightning

Silver Lightning was the fastest train on the tracks. His engine was shining silver with blue and red flashes down the side.

On journeys, Silver Lightning sped from city to city so fast, that all folks saw when he whizzed past, was a blur........

"What an amazing train." the passengers said. "Silver Lightning can drive himself - he doesn't need a driver or a guard!"

"But I do!" cried Silver Lightning, and a big tear rolled down his gleaming paintwork. "I'm so lonely all by myself!"

So the man in charge of the railway found Silver Lightning his own driver and his own guard, who had nothing to do but ride everywhere on the special silver train and keep him happy!

Three Busy Workmen

Three busy workmen were digging a very deep hole in the road, when quite by accident their drill hit a water-pipe.

Soon everything was soaking wet and water was spurting in all directions.

"How on earth did that happen?" asked Jim

"I think it was my fault!" said John.

"Can't be helped," said Joe "let's have our lunch!"

So the three busy workmen sat down and opened their lunch-boxes.

"Oh dear!" groaned Jim as he took out rulers and pencils and felt-tipped pens. "I've picked up my little girl's school-case by mistake!"

Then John opened his lunch box, and he'd picked up the wrong case as well - it was packed full of his little boy's school-books.

"I'd better look in mine," laughed Joe, and he began to blush. His wife had handed Joe her make-up case by mistake, with all her lipsticks and hairsprays!

"This means we have no lunch at all! cried the three busy workmen.

"If you promise to mend the pipe and stop all the water leaking," shouted the man from the sandwich shop nearby, "I'll make lunch for all three of you!"...........and the three busy workmen did just that!

The Bathroom Battle

Peter's mum was in a hurry one night at bathtime.

She rubbed and scrubbed Peter in double quick time, before he could blink he was washed, dried and tucked up tight in bed..........

.........back in the bathroom, all the toys were left alone on the shelf.

"It's not fair," said the penguin, "no-one has had time to play with us in the bath tonight!"

"Does that mean we shan't get bathed until tomorrow?" quacked the yellow duck.

"I love bath water!" cried the little blue fish. "Especially when it's full of bubbles."

"So do I!" barked the seal. "I hate being dry."

"Then we must do something about it!" the toy sailor said as he stood on the edge of the bath and spoke to them all. "I can turn on the taps, but I need a little help."

"I can use the end of my tail," said the whale. "I'll turn on the hot tap and you can do the cold tap," he told the sailor.

"Plug's in the plug-hole!" said the little blue fish, as he swam quickly out of the way of the hot water.

It wasn't long before the bath was almost full. The seal put his flipper into the water - just to make sure that it wasn't too hot for the toys.

When the penguin gave the signal everyone dived in, and the sailor very kindly launched the boats and a whole family of ducks into the bath water.

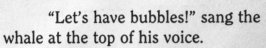

"Let's have bubbles!" sang the whale at the top of his voice.

"Better still," barked the seal as he dived beneath the water, "let's have a bubble battle!"

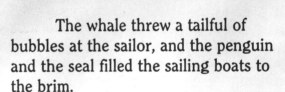

Pretty soon everywhere was covered in soft white foam. There were big blobs of bubbles on the bathroom walls, and a pool of water all over the floor.

The whale threw a tailful of bubbles at the sailor, and the penguin and the seal filled the sailing boats to the brim.

"Quiet, someones coming!" yelled the sailor. Quick as a flash, the little blue fish dived down and pulled out the plug.

"This bathroom's been left a mess!" said Peter's dad as he opened the door. "Better get it cleaned up before Mum sees it!"

So he dried all the toys and put them back on the shelf.

The penguin, who was standing next to the seal, gave him a little nudge. "How about another bathroom battle tomorrow night?" he said.

Harriet's Wish

"I wish I had a playhouse." said Harriet one day. "Then I could sit inside and just pretend!" and off she went.

"Did you hear that?" whispered her dad.

"I did!" replied Harriet's mum just as quietly.

"If Harriet wants a playhouse, I shall build her one!" said her dad, quite determined.

So away he hurried to buy lots of wood, and to see if he needed any new tools.

"Are you sure Harriet really wants a playhouse?" mum shouted after him. But dad was already on his way to the timber yard.

It took simply ages to build the playhouse, with dad hammering and banging in nails every time Harriet left the house.

At long last it was finished, and mum and dad called Harriet into the garden to take a look.

Harriet was speechless and held her breath for a very long time, which made her mum look worried.

14

"That's not what I wanted!" cried Harriet shaking her head. So she ran indoors and came back with a picture of her playhouse in a book.

"Is that all" gasped her dad as he fell back into a garden chair.

"I want a playhouse just like that!" said the little girl, and she held up the book.........

.........Now Harriet has the playhouse she really wanted - and dad has a brand new toolshed that he built himself!

The Penguins Join The Party

Chrissy, Sissy and Missy were sisters. They lived with their brother Sidney on an iceberg in the Atlantic Ocean.

One day a ship taking passengers on a cruise stopped right next to the penguin's iceberg.

The people on board the cruise-ship had never seen penguins before, especially one in a red waistcoat! So they leaned over the side and began to take video films and photographs.

"Do you mind being stared at?" Chrissy, Sissy and Missy asked their brother Sidney.

"Not one bit!" said Sidney as he straightened his bow-tie.

So the four little penguins posed for the cameras until it grew dark.

Late that night, Chrissy, Sissy, Missy and Sidney heard music.......it came from the brightly lit cruise-ship.

"Come on girls!" said Sidney. "It sounds like a party, so let's join in!"

So Chrissy, Sissy, Missy and Sidney jumped off their iceberg, swam over to the ship and clambered up on deck.

"Welcome aboard!" yelled the captain above the noise. "Today we stared at you, now it's your turn to stare at us. Come and join the party!"

Randolph the Reindeer was extremely shy. While the other reindeer trotted through the trees holding their heads high and tossing their antlers from side to side - Randolph stood quietly nibbling the moss on the ground, with his head down.

Randolph The Reindeer

"You're too timid, Randolph!" bellowed the other reindeer as they leapt through the woods. "Be a show-off like us!"

But Randolph pretended not to hear, he just went on nibbling the moss on the ground with his head down.

Then from beyond the trees came the shouts of children as they tobogganed down the snowy hillside.

"I'd love to join in," sighed Randolph, "but I'm far too shy!"

Then as Randolph began to nibble the moss on the ground with his head down, he came across a woollen hat. Next he found a mitten, then a long scarf.

18

All at once Randolph's nose began to twitch, and without thinking he held his head high and began to look around.........there in a clearing on the edge of the trees lay a little boy by the side of his toboggan.

"I've hurt my leg and I can't walk!" the little boy cried.

This made Randolph feel so proud, that he lifted up his head and tossed his antlers from side to side - just like the other reindeer!

So Randolph knelt down, and the little boy slipped his arms round the reindeer's neck and climbed on his back.

Very soon he was back home safely, thanks to Randolph.

"You're a hero!" said the little boy.

The Baby Bird's Bedtime

It was late afternoon and all the baby birds were practising flying.

"I can fly upside-down!" chirped a young robin.

"Can you dive from the top of the poplar tree, then brake just before you hit the ground?" asked one daring little thrush who had tried it several times.

"Look at us!" cried nine of the tiniest sparrows, as they flew close together overhead.

Just then, a strange little beak and two big eyes appeared from inside the trunk of the poplar tree.

"Hi everybody!" said a squeaky little voice. "I'm Ollie, can I play with you?

The baby birds stopped what they were doing at once and gathered around.

"You're new here" chirped the robin.

"Not exactly," Ollie replied. "I live in that hollow tree, and I've been here all the time."

"It's getting rather late for you to play." said one of the bluebirds. "Soon it will be dark!"

Poor Ollie looked very disappointed as he had just made so many new friends.

Then all of a sudden he thought of a wonderful idea.

"Why not stay over with me tonight?" cried Ollie.

So off flew the little birds and came back wearing pyjamas. (One or two of the really young ones brought their blankets and pillows.)

"It's so exciting," sang the robin. "I've never stayed up all night before!"

At first everything went wonderfully well. The baby birds fluttered in and out of the branches, playing tag in the twilight.

But when darkness fell, they kept bumping into one another, and the thrush almost fell off his perch onto the ground below!

Ollie could see that his new friends were getting rather tired, so off he flew and came back with a tray of snacks and nice things to nibble.

"We're having a midnight feast!" whispered one of the sparrows, his head nodding onto his pillow.

Soon all the baby birds were falling asleep.........some of them looked really uncomfortable.

"Why are you still wide awake, Ollie? the robin asked drowsily.

"It's because I'm an OWL, and we stay up all night long!" smiled Ollie........and he took all the sleepy little birds back to their warm nests.

Gordon's New House

Gordon the Gorilla was looking for a new house. So he rang up the man who sold really nice houses.

As you can see the house turned out to be a bit on the small side for Gordon.

I think that Gordon forgot to tell the man who sold really nice houses, that he was a gorilla.

"I have the perfect place for you, Mr Gordon." said the man who sold really nice houses. "It has a bright red roof, two tall chimneys and a smart white fence."

"Sounds just the job!" grunted Gordon.

"If you like it, Mr Gordon," said the man who sold really nice houses, "I'll be round straight away and you can pay me all your money!"

Belinda, The Circus Star

"I'm off to join the circus and be a star!" announced Belinda the ragdoll one morning at breakfast.

"For ever?" gasped the soldier doll.

"No silly!" Belinda sniffed. "Just for one day."

"One day!" all the toys laughed out loud. "How can you be a circus star in just one day?"

"Easy," said Belinda, "the clowns will teach me, you see!" and off she went.

At first the clowns were thrilled to see Belinda, because they thought the ragdoll was charming and very, very pretty, and every single one of the clowns wanted to teach her their tricks.

"I don't want to do tricks." said Belinda quite snappy. "I want to walk a tight-rope!"

"A tight-rope?" this surprised all the clowns.

"How about juggling instead?" asked one of them.

"Riding a unicycle is good fun!" suggested another.

Then all the clowns stood in front of Belinda. "We should never allow a beautiful ragdoll like yourself, to swing on a trapeze, or ride bareback, or walk a tight-rope - it's far too dangerous.........and that's final!" they shouted.

"Rubbish!" Belinda yelled back as she stamped her feet. "I've already told my friends that I am going to walk a tight-rope and be a star......and that's final too!"

Whatever was to be done?

The clowns liked Belinda very much and didn't want to disappoint her, in spite of her bad temper that day.

"There is one way you can learn to walk the tight-rope without being in any danger at all!" said the clown with the big feet.

"Show me! Show me! Do, do, do!" shouted Belinda, very impatient.....and so they did!

Belinda the ragdoll walked up and down the tight-rope all that day. She wore sparkling tights and a silver star on her head.......and when the toys came to call for her that night, she showed them what she could do. "But Belinda," said the toys, "your tight-rope is only a few inches off the ground!" and they all burst out laughing!

"I agree," and Belinda smiled her prettiest and most charming smile, "but I did learn to walk a tight-rope and I am a circus star!"..........then she bowed, still wearing her sparkling tights and silver star!

The Bear Who Drove The School Bus

On certain days when the regular driver had a day off, Barnaby would drive the school bus.

Now on those days when Barnaby drove the bus to school, he picked up his young animal friends at stops all along the forest road.

One day, as his last passenger climbed aboard, Barnaby got back into the driving seat - and the bus would not start.

However hard Barnaby tried, he could not start the engine!

"Hurrah!" yelled one of the raccoon twins. "Let's take the day off!"

So before Barnaby could stop them, all the young animals had jumped off the bus and rushed into the woods to play hide and seek.

"This is very naughty of you all!" shouted Barnaby, trying to sound gruff. "Come back at once!" and his voice echoed through the trees.

All the rest of that morning, poor Barnaby ran round in circles trying to catch the young animals. Every so often he would glimpse a couple of them peeking from behind a tree trunk.

Time passed and Barnaby began to feel hungry. "It must be almost dinner time!" he said out loud.

27

Then, as if from nowhere, all Barnaby's little animal passengers appeared.

"I'm very hungry!" cried one little fox cub.

"I'm hungry and thirsty too!" said a small squirrel.

"Take us back to school for our dinner!" the animals shouted all at once.

"I might have some food in my bag," said Barnaby, as he led them back to the bus - but all he could find was a packet of cough sweets and some rather old biscuits.

"We want our dinner!" "We want our dinner!" the animals began to chant, and they banged their feet loudly on the bus floor.

Just at that moment, a big car-transporter drew alongside the school bus.

"Need a lift?" asked the driver.

"I need lots of lifts" laughed Barnaby.

So Barnaby and the driver put a few of the animals into each car on the transporter.

"First stop school!" shouted the driver.

"Just in time for dinner!" yelled the little animals.

29

Dottie's In Fashion

Winter was coming and the weather was getting colder, so Dottie the dormouse went to the store to buy a new coat.

"Choose something sensible that is comfortable and warm." suggested her cousin Dora.

"Not likely!" scoffed Dottie. "My new coat will be the latest fashion!"...........then Dottie saw it.......... the most fashionable coat in the whole world!

"I'll take it!" Dottie yelled at the top of her voice. "Wrap it up at once!"

"Aren't you going to try it on?" asked her cousin Dora as she gazed open-mouthed at Dottie's new coat. "It looks rather thin!"

But Dottie didn't hear her, she was far too busy trying on a pair of high-heeled boots to match.

"They look very unsuitable for wet, winter weather." said Dora under her breath as she followed Dottie out of the store.

During the night it turned very cold. The north wind blew and it started to snow, and it went on snowing and snowing and snowing.

When Dottie and Dora looked out of their window the next morning, the whole world was white.

"Get a move on Dottie!" cried Dora, who was already dressed in her warm jacket and boots.

I'll need time to button my coat up!" snapped Dottie. "Then it will take me quite a while to lace up my boots!"

So Dora went out to play in the snow with her friends.

At long last Dottie was ready. She stepped outside in her high-heeled fashionable boots and fell flat on her back!

Now Dora and her friends were having a great time throwing snowballs and building a snowman. But the snow was cold and wet, and very soon poor Dottie felt frozen in her fashionable coat.

"It's so c-c-c-cold, and my t-t-t-toes ache!"

"Let's get you inside." said cousin Dora shaking her head. "You need warm clothes on a day like this, not fashionable ones!"

"You're right!" agreed Dottie as she thawed out in front of a warm fire.

"Tomorrow we'll both go shopping and you can choose some sensible clothes for me Dora......and I'll pack my fashionable coat and boots away until spring!"

Mat's Coffee Morning

Mat the Bat was feeling lonely. "I need to make new friends." he squeaked as he flitted across the night sky.

"My problem is," he told a passing owl, "each time I introduce myself, everyone screams and runs away!"

"I understand," nodded the owl wisely. "When people see a bat they think of witches and broomsticks and Halloween."

"Got it in one!" piped Mat. "They think of skeletons with rattling bones, and ghosts that jump out at you and shriek and groan!"

"Enough!" hooted the owl. "You're scaring me stiff!"

"Didn't mean too!" said Mat the Bat. "But what can I do?"

"Have a coffee morning!" suggested the owl. "Put a notice on your door inviting anyone passing to come in for coffee and cake. But remember, be sure to have it in the daytime!"

"What a clever old owl you are!" and Mat the Bat smiled as he flitted off home......

.........now when visitors came to Mat's house the next day to join him for coffee and cake - they were in for a surprise.

There was Mat in his neat little house serving coffee and cake in his best frilly apron....UPSIDE-DOWN...... but don't forget that Mat's a bat!

Buggy Races

"Would you like to race me down to the beach?" the Hare asked the Tortoise.

"Not really," muttered the Tortoise. "You'll win as usual!"

"That's true," said the Hare in a kind voice. "I'm sorry you always lose, it can't be much fun!"

But one day, the Hare found a way to race the Tortoise that would be fair and lots of fun too.

Come and look what I have found?" called the Hare to the Tortoise, who was slowly plodding over the sandhill towards the beach.

Now the two friends can race against each other all day......and something tells me that the Tortoise might win this time.........

Gussie The Ginger Cat

Gussie the Ginger Cat made up her mind one day to catch every single mouse in the house.

So she fetched the biggest, tastiest, smelliest piece of cheese she could find, and put it inside a bag.

Now Gussie's bag had a string round the top. "When this bag is full of mice," sniggered Gussie, "I shall pull the string so tightly, that not one of them will escape."

But what Gussie didn't know, was that her bag had a big hole in the bottom.

So one by one, the crafty mice scampered into the bag, picked up the cheese and carried it out through the hole at the other end.

"Better luck next time Gussie!" giggled the mice, their mouths full of tasty cheese.

Matching Hats

Four tiny fieldmice went to playschool for the very first time.

"I want to paint!" said the first one.

"I want to make a model!" said the second.

"I want to sing and dance!" said the third.

"And I want milk and biscuits!" said the fourth.

While they were at playschool, each one of the tiny fieldmice had painted a picture, made a model, had danced round in a ring and sung a song about a farmer.

And all four tiny fieldmice had eaten a plateful of iced biscuits and shared a glass of milk with four curly straws.

At last it was time to go home, and the four tiny fieldmice went to find their hats.

"That's not my hat!" shouted the first one.

"That's not my hat!" shouted the second.

That's not my hat!" shouted the third.

"Our hats must match!" shouted the fourth.

So can you help the fieldmice sort out their hats? They really are in a muddle!

The Farmer's Barn

One fine morning in autumn, a farmer and his wife were strolling through the fields looking at their corn crop.

"We've never had such a good harvest, dear!" said the farmer happily. "There'll be plenty of corn for us and all our friends. In fact, there'll be enough left over to feed the birds through the long winter."

"We'll give a party." suggested the farmer's wife. "In fact, my dear, I'll ask my cousins from over the hills and faraway."

So the farmer and his wife sent out invitations. Then they got busy in the farmhouse kitchen and made lots of delicious things to eat.

They set the food out in one of their fields under the shade of a tree.

Soon neighbours began to arrive, and last of all came the cousins from over the hills and faraway.

It wasn't very long before everyone tucked into the lovely food and seemed to be having a good time.

It was then the farmer and his wife noticed that the cousins from over the hill and faraway looked a bit glum.

"Whatever is the matter?" asked the farmer.

"There must be something wrong with my food!" said the farmer's wife, and she tasted a piece of pie to make sure.

"The food is fine, thank you," the cousins from over the hills and faraway replied quietly. "But this year our crops have failed, and we have no corn to eat or save in our barns for winter."

"Don't worry!" cried the farmer. "There's plenty here for all. Take as much as you like home with you, and then come back for more!"

At this, the cousins from over the hills and faraway cheered up considerably and began to enjoy the party.

When, at last, the food was finished and all the pots cleared away, the cousins from over the hills and faraway took a stroll round the farm...and would you believe it, for the second time that day, their faces began to look glum.

"Look at your barns," they said to the farmer and his wife. "They're falling to bits, you'll have nowhere to store your corn this winter!"

Now it was the farmer's turn to look glum.

"Not to worry!" said the cousins from over the hills and faraway. "We'll stay a few days and repair your barns for you. It will be our way of saying thank you for giving us the corn.

The Tired Little Monkey

The smallest monkey at the zoo was very fond of Norah, the zoo-keeper's wife.

"It's because you spoil him so much," the zoo keeper grinned.

"I can't help it," Norah smiled as she lifted the little monkey up in her arms. "He's so cuddly and sweet, and he's just a baby!"

Now the little monkey liked nothing better than to follow Norah around all day long as she worked in the zoo.

"Can you carry me?" the little monkey asked Norah one afternoon. "My legs are tired!"

So for the rest of that afternoon, Norah took the little monkey around the zoo on her back.

"I do like this!" cried the little monkey. "I can see everything from up here, and I'm not a bit tired!"

"But I am!" whispered Norah under her breath (because she didn't want to upset the little monkey).

It took poor Norah twice as long to do all her jobs in the zoo, because the little monkey kept hugging her tightly round the neck and tickling her ears.

"Can we do this everyday?" begged the little monkey, and Norah gave a big sigh......

.........early next morning the zoo keeper went into town to buy a pushchair - it was Norah's idea!

So now that little monkey is pushed around the zoo. He never gets tired, and neither does Norah!

Pippin Has The Measles

Ma and Pa Bramley were looking rather worried. Pippin, their pet pig, felt poorly.

"Have you been eating green apples from my orchard?" asked Pa.

"Not one!" sniffed poor Pippin.

"Have you been drinking from muddy puddles?" asked Ma, because she had often watched Pippin do this when she thought no one was looking.

"We must send for the doctor," Ma and Pa decided, "he'll be sure to know what's the matter!"

By the time the doctor arrived, Pippin was covered in tiny red spots.

"Measles!" the doctor nodded wisely. "You have a pig with the measles!"

"You must stay in the kitchen with me!" announced Ma Bramley. "Then you will be warm and dry, and I can make sure that you have plenty of warm bread and milk with brown

40

sugar on top!"

Pippin quite liked the sound of this, so she trotted into Ma Bramley's kitchen and settled down in front of the fire.

It wasn't long before Pippin the pig began to feel a bit better, although she was still covered in bright red spots.

Some of the children in the valley heard about their friend Pippin and came to see how she was feeling.

"It's good to see you all," snuffled Pippin as she trotted towards the kitchen door.

"STOP RIGHT WHERE YOU ARE!" cried Ma Bramley. "You'll have all these nice children covered in spots and in no time at all the whole valley will catch the measles!"

"Did the doctor say when I could go out?" asked Pippin.

"Exactly one week from now, and not a moment before!" replied Ma Bramley with a very determined look in her eye.

This news made Pippin look very glum. "Does that mean I can't see my friends for a whole week?" cried the little pig.

"Not at all!" chuckled Pa Bramley as he came in from his orchard.

"I've made you a gate from the branches of an old apple tree. You can stay in the kitchen on one side of the gate, and your friends can stay on the other. That way you'll be happy, and your friends won't catch the measles!"

"We will come and see Pippin every day until her spots have disappeared!" cried the children. "Thanks a lot Pa Bramley!"

Plumber Bear's Good Idea

Nanni Bear was having her breakfast early one morning, when she felt a drop of water fall onto her head, and when she looked up at the ceiling, another one splashed onto her nose.

"There must be a leak in the bathroom!" said Nanni as she pushed the teapot into the middle of the table to catch the drips.

"I'll send for Plumber Bear straight away. He'll know what to do!"

When Plumber Bear came at long last, he went straight upstairs. As he walked out of the bathroom he shook his head.

"You need a new bath, and a new wash-basin and a new toilet. Your bath is leaking, your wash-basin is cracked and your toilet is very old-fashioned!"

"No wonder," said Nanni Bear, "they must be at least as old as me. You'd better put in a new bathroom!"

"It will take quite a while," said Plumber Bear. "You never know what I might find!"

So off went Nanni to stay with her sister for a week until the work was done.

When she returned, there was Plumber Bear standing in the garden looking very pleased with himself.

"I know you were fond of your old bathroom so I didn't throw it away," he said grinning and pointing to a corner of the garden. "Here it is!"........how Nanni Bear laughed when she saw what Plumber Bear had done!

What Hideous Creatures

One sunny day, a very forgetful professor got down on a grassy bank and began to look at the insects through his magnifying glass.

Now when the professor left for home, he forgot all about his magnifying glass, so straight away all the insects gathered round.

"This is just the thing we need!" and they jumped for joy.

"When the birds fly down to gobble us up, we'll give them a fright for a change!".........and so they did.

The birds had never seen such hideous creatures. They took off squawking with fright and never flew down again!

Helga's Toe

Helga the Hippo went for a walk one day. The sky was blue and the sun was warm.

"What a lovely day for a stroll!" bellowed Helga as she thundered along flattening everything in her path.

Now Helga was a particularly huge and heavy hippo, and when she was on the move, everybody got out of her way!

Suddenly as Helga thudded by, a teeny tiny insect stepped on her toe.

"Why can't you pick on someone your own size?" howled Helga as she limped off home!

Huey's Present

Huey the Hairy Caterpillar was looking for a present for his girlfriend.

"Does she like lettuce?" asked a passing ant.

"A lettuce leaf isn't much of a present!" said Huey. "And it's not very romantic!"

"How about a fresh spring onion?" suggested a brightly coloured beetle.

"Now you're just being silly," and Huey groaned as he wriggled away.

"Take her one perfect flower!" a butterfly sighed as she fluttered by.

And straight away, Huey knew that was the right idea.

So he picked a beautiful yellow daisy and crawled off to visit his girlfriend.

"How very romantic!" sighed Huey's girlfriend as she gazed at the flower, then they sat together in the warm sun..........and ate it!

Rain, Rain, Go Away!

"What a beautiful day," called the youngest grey rabbit as he took a look outside.

"The weather forecast is rain later," said Mrs Grey Rabbit as she hurried to finish her washing.

"Let's go on a picnic," suggested one of the older rabbits, "then we'll be out of Mother's way for a while!"

Although Mrs Rabbit had to admit that this was a good idea, she made all the young rabbits promise to take a rug or cushion in case the grass was damp, and an umbrella or jacket because rain was forecast.

So the little grey rabbits each packed a picnic basket full of their favourite nibbles and set off down the lane.

As they marched along swinging their picnic baskets, they sang at the tops of their voices,
"Rain, rain, go away,
Come again another day."

The sun shone brightly all that morning. The little grey rabbits played games in the fields, and at lunchtime they set out their picnic on the grass.

Just as they had finished the last mouthful, the wind blew a big black cloud over their heads and it began to rain.

"Oh dear!" cried the little rabbits all together. "We remembered our picnic baskets, but we forgot our umbrellas and our jackets!"

"Never mind," said one of the rabbits, "we can still keep dry on the way home!"........and this is how they did it........as they ran through the raindrops they sang at the tops of their voices,

"Rain on the green grass,
And rain on the tree,
And rain on the housetop,
But not on me!"

Mrs Grey Rabbit was looking out of the window anxious for her family to return. When she saw them coming down the lane, she had to smile.

"That's one way of keeping dry!" she laughed as she hurried them inside out of the rain.

"Rain, rain, go away,
Come on Mother's washing day!"

Lolli And Pop's New Car

Lolli and Pop took out all their savings from the bank and bought a new car.

They parked it in front of their garden gate and for the rest of the day, Lolli and Pop gazed out of the window admiring it.

"Let's go for a ride," said Lolli to Pop next morning. So after breakfast they locked up the house, went down the garden path, Pop got into the driving seat of their shiny new car and turned the key.

"Please start!" said Pop to the little car.

"No" came the reply.

"Please will you take us for a ride?" Lolli asked.

"Won't!" snapped the car.

Would you believe it........every day the same thing happened. However many times Pop tried to start the car, it simply would not budge.

"It's no good," said Lolli to Pop, "we shall just have to stay at home!"

As time went by, Lolli and Pop's shiny new car began to get dirty parked on the dusty road. The tyres were flat and a careless boy on a bike put a dent in the wing. One of the doors was scratched and the bonnet was covered in muddy paw-prints made by next door's cat.

"Our little car is only fit for the scrapyard now," said Lolli to Pop as they leaned over the garden gate.

"What's that I hear?" gasped the little car feeling quite shocked. "I've been very stupid parked here sulking all this time. I don't want to be sent to the scrapyard!"

So he tried very hard to start his engine. The little car coughed and spluttered, but try as he might, his engine simply would not start!

Lolli and Pop heard their little car and rushed over to help.

Pop threw open the bonnet and tinkered with the engine. Lolli pumped up the tyres then washed and waxed the paintwork.

"I'm afraid you'll have to go to the garage to have that dent in your wing put right," said Pop.

So the two of them jumped into the little car and Pop turned the key.

"Please start!" said Pop to the little car, and the motor began to tick over at once.

"Please will you take us for a ride?" asked Lolli - and off they raced.

49

Mantu's Little Elephant

Little Mantu lived in a village deep in the jungle where elephants helped the men with their work.

These elephants were so big and strong, they could lift up the heaviest logs with their trunks and toss them high in the air.

Most of the elephants were great show-offs, and Mantu often told them so.

Now, Mantu had an elephant of his very own. His name was Opie. He was just a baby, and Mantu's much loved pet.

"One day when you grow up," Mantu whispered in his Opie's ear, "you'll be the biggest, strongest and bravest elephant in the jungle."

Now the herd of elephants, who had very big ears, heard what Mantu had whispered to Opie.

They began to laugh and stamp their feet and make very rude noises with their long trunks.

"You'll never grow up to be as big as us!" they screeched, and they filled their trunks with water and wet Opie through.

"You're so small, you're nothing at all!" the big elephants chorused rudely.

"We're so tall, we can see over the trees and far away." one sneered. "In fact, we can see snow sparkling on the tops of the mountains!" and he trumpeted loudly in Opie's ear.

"Is that a fact?" whispered Opie quietly, feeling very small indeed.

"Don't worry!" smiled Mantu throwing both arms round his elephant. "I'm small too, we'll soon grow!"

Then Mantu looked up at the huge elephants with a mischievous glint in his eye.

"Although you are very tall and can see over the treetops. We can see what is happening down here in the jungle...........In fact we would be the first to see any long, slithering snakes that may be about to coil themselves round your legs!"

"Snakes!" screeched the elephants. "Did you say long, slithering snakes?" and off they thundered in fright.

"Did I say there were snakes?" giggled Mantu.

"No, you most definitely did not!" smiled Opie.

And Mantu climbed upon his little friends back and went home to the village to tell everyone about the foolish elephants.

Mr Merry's Brilliant Ideas

It was Mr Merry's birthday and his wife bought him the very latest computer, designed for very clever people only.

"Brilliant!" cried Mr Merry. "I am a very clever person, so I shall sit down at my shiny new computer and begin inventing things straight away.

In the very first hour, Mr Merry invented square wheels.

"No-one has ever thought of square wheels before," chuckled Mr Merry.

"I must be a genius!"

So he fixed them onto Baby Merry's pram. Half-way down the road she got hiccups...........so Mr Merry went back to his computer.

It didn't take Mr Merry too long before he came up with another amazing invention.........the automatic supermarket trolley.

"No-one will ever have to push a trolley full of shopping again!" announced Mr Merry - and he was absolutely right.

The automatic trolley whizzed round the supermarket in all directions. It crashed into the displays and shopping flew everywhere.

So poor Mr Merry went back to his computer..........soon new ideas came thick and fast. In less time than it takes to count to ten, he had invented blow-up trousers, spring-loaded trainers and an extremely high powered hair-dryer.

Mrs Merry felt that enough was enough. Very quietly she crept over to the computer and pulled out the plug.

"Dear, oh dear!" said Mr Merry puzzled. "I do believe my new computer has broken!"

"Never mind," said Mrs Merry as she sighed with relief. "I think you've invented enough for one day, you can help me with dinner."

"Ace!" cried Mr Merry as he rushed into the kitchen. "I'm brilliant at inventing new dishes. Sit down, dear," he told Mrs Merry, "I'll have the meal cooked in a jiffy!"

So that night, when dinner was ready, Mr and Mrs Merry tucked in to..........chocolate fish fingers, striped mashed potatoes, purple peas, and a glass of Mr Merry's special fizz-a-lot coke!

A Lick Of Paint

The animals from the toy farm were looking very shabby indeed.

"I once had brown spots," moaned the cow, "look at me now, my paint has peeled off and I'm just plain wood!"

"My feathers used to be all the colours of the rainbow," the turkey sighed.

"I was just as bright as you," crowed the cockerel, "in fact my feathers were even more colourful!"

"Now stop all that arguing!" scolded the sheep as he looked across at the other animals. "All of us are dull and shabby, every one of us could do with a lick of paint."

"Just a minute," cried one of the toys, "there are some paints in the toy box. Let's find some brushes and brighten up the farm animals."

Several of the toys set to work straight away.

It wasn't as easy as they thought. Some of the farm animals fidgeted and wouldn't stand still. The pony kept tossing his head and two of the lambs knocked over the paint pots.

At last the toys finished, but when they stepped back to admire their work, they got an awful shock.

"You've given me purple spots and green feet!" cried the cow.

"I'm all streaky and striped!" gasped the pony.

"You look a sight!" gobbled the turkey when he saw the cockerel.

"You look even worse!" squawked the cockerel in reply.

"Stop arguing," cried the rag-doll. "This paint will wash off, or so it says on the jar."

So the rag-doll and several of the other toys fetched bowls of soapy water and sponges, and after much rubbing and scrubbing, the farm animals were back to their plain old boring colour once more......

..........and so they stayed, until Great Uncle Percy came to visit the family.

He took one look in the toy box, spied the farm animals and said in a loud voice. "What a shabby lot, you could do with a lick of paint!"

Now Great Uncle Percy knew a thing or two about animals, he also knew how to paint.........as you can see from the results!

Paddy The Park-Keeper

One weekend in March the park was closed for a spring clean and Paddy was very busy.

"I'm pleased this just happens just once a year," said Paddy. "The grown-ups don't like the park gates locked and the children hate it!"

So during the next two days Paddy and his helpers went round the park picking up the litter, they weeded the flower-beds and painted all the swings and roundabouts in bright colours.

"Before the park opens tomorrow morning," Paddy told his helpers, "we must be sure to put up notices that say WET PAINT next to the swings and park benches that we've painted."

Then Paddy asked his hard-working helpers if they would like to join him for a cup of tea before they went home.

So they all sat together on a bench in the sunshine and enjoyed a well-earned break............but when they got up to go, every single one of them was covered in wet paint.

"Oh dear," said Paddy, "we should have put the WET PAINT notices out before we sat down!"

The Spooky Old Tree

Mr Badger was strolling through the woods one day when he came across a spooky looking old tree.

"Goodness me!" gasped Mr Badger. "That spooky old tree gave me a real shock."

"Everyone says that!" grumbled a deep voice from down inside the tree's trunk.

"Who said that?" cried Mr Badger glancing around.

"Can't you see?" said the voice. "It's me, the tree!"

Because Mr Badger looked so kind and wise, the tree explained how lonely he was all by himself in the wood.

"I'll admit that I look spooky and scary," the tree told Mr Badger, "but all I need is a bit of company. Perhaps a few animals could come and live in my trunk, and one or two birds might come and nest in my branches."

57

"I think I can arrange that," said Mr Badger with a chuckle. "I have a few friends who are looking for a new home - but they can be quite a handful at times, and they make plenty of noise!"

"Bring them along please," begged the tree, "as soon as you can!"

First of all Mr Badger cleared a space round the tree's great trunk. Then he made new paths that led out of the woods, and edged them with white painted stones.

"I'll put up a light or two before it gets dark, then you'll not look so spooky or scary."

The tree was beginning to enjoy all this attention.

In the next day or so lots of the badger's woodland friends came to visit the tree.

"We would like to make our home in your hollow trunk," said a family of squirrels, "if it's not too much to ask."

"You can have your own flat, right at the top!" laughed the tree, who by now was wearing a big beaming smile.

"Can I have a home too? Twit Twoo!" hooted an owl.

"Please let us dig burrows in your roots!" begged the rabbits.

"Is there room for us in your branches?" cawed the rooks at the tops of their voices.

"I told you some of my friends were a bit noisy." said Mr Badger as he leaned on the tree's trunk.

"I don't mind one little bit," the tree beamed with pleasure," I shall never be lonely again, thanks to you Badger!"

58

Edwin The Engine

It was snowing quite hard when the engine driver put Edwin the Engine back in his shed after his last journey of the day.

"I think it will snow all night long!" said the engine driver to the guard.

"I've never seen such big snowflakes!" shouted the ticket collector as he looked out of the window.

Very soon the snow was so thick that it covered the station carpark.

"We can't get home tonight," announced the driver.

"Then we'll have to stay here with Edwin!" said the guard and the ticket collector both in the same breath.

So they lit the stove and cooked sausages and beans and made a large pot of coffee.

"It's like camping out!" laughed the guard.

"But much better!" replied the driver and ticket collector as they made themselves comfortable for the night.

As for Edwin the Engine, he thought this was great fun. He enjoyed having company in his train shed. "It's just like an adventure!" he hooted as he dropped off to sleep.

Next morning the snow was so deep, that the railway men couldn't open Edwin's shed doors.

"You'll have to push them open Edwin!" said the driver, so the train drove straight into the doors. "Push Edwin! Push with all your might!"

At last the doors burst open and Edwin chugged slowly out into the sunshine.

What a sight met their eyes! The snow had drifted during the night and had almost covered the station and most of the town too.

A few brave people had struggled through the snow and were standing on the platform waiting for Edwin.

"We need your help Edwin." said the worried station-master. "You're the only one that can get through to the farms and houses along the track.

Very soon the baker and grocer were loading boxes of food into Edwin's carriages.

"Can you drop these off to the folks who live by the side of the railway line?" asked the station-master.

"Certainly!" tooted Edwin blowing his whistle loudly.

"Will you take this hay to the cattle and bring back the newborn lambs - so we can find a warm place for them?" went on the worried station-master, who by this time looked like a snowman.

"I'll do my best," replied Edwin as he chugged very slowly out of the station.

It wasn't easy ploughing through the thick snowdrifts, in fact it needed every bit of power in Edwin's engine.

The folks along the track were delighted with the fresh bread and milk and all the food that Edwin had brought them.

"You're a hero!" said one farmer as he loaded his tiny lambs into Edwin's warm carriage. "My lambs will be safe now!"

The snow was so deep that it lasted a long, long time. For weeks Edwin took the children too and from school. He brought people fresh bread every morning and big bags of logs for their fires.

When at last the snow melted, everyone felt they should thank Edwin, for looking after them so well.

So on the very first day that the weather was fine, they all gathered at the station and presented Edwin with a brass plaque to go on the front of his engine.

Edwin wears it proudly to this day.....and if you should happen to see an engine with a special brass plaque.....take a good look - it could be Edwin!

William's Monsters

William had a very vivid imagination...........he thought he saw monsters everywhere.........and sometimes he would just pretend he did!

When he was walking to school in the morning, he would shout out loudly. "Look at that monster peeping over the fence - he's coming after you!"

"Don't be so silly William!" shouted one of the girls in his class.

She didn't turn round or even bother to look, she just walked on.

"Watch out!" screamed William as he ran after his classmates. "They're crawling out of cracks in the pavement.........there are monsters everywhere!"

But no one ever took the slightest notice of William.

As soon as he returned home

William pretended to see monsters in the kitchen and monsters in the hall, he even said he saw them sitting on the stairs.

At bedtime he shouted to his Mum and Dad that there was a monster in the bath and another down the toilet.

"I'm getting very tired of this," said Dad as he turned on the television.

"Don't worry," said Mum with a smile, "He'll grow out of it!"

That night when she went upstairs to tuck William in, she said, "Have you noticed the monster that's crept into your bed?"

William almost jumped out of his skin........after a while his Mum began to laugh.

"You're the little monster William!" she said as she kissed him goodnight!

Warning Lights

Darkness was falling and it was getting late. Lolli and Pop said goodnight to their little car parked by the garden gate, then went inside to get ready for bed.

They hadn't been asleep very long before something woke Lolli up.

"There's a strange light!" whispered Lolli as she shook Pop's arm.

"If I get up and take a look," sighed Pop getting out of bed, "promise we can go back to sleep!"

Now when Pop looked out of the window, he was surprised to see two bright lights flashing outside.

"Perhaps a spaceship has landed in our garden!" gasped Lolli.

"Nonsense!" said Pop. "It's our little car flashing his headlights. Something must be wrong."

As quick as could be, Lolli and Pop ran downstairs and out into the garden in their nightclothes.

"Look!" cried Lolli grabbing Pop's arm. "Our garden fence is on fire!"

"Goodness, gracious me!" cried Pop. "Our little car has tried to warn us by flashing his lights."

"Send for the fire-brigade at once!" Lolli screamed.

"A couple of buckets of water will do nicely!" said Pop calmly. "We don't need to turn out the fire-engine at this time of night."

So Lolli and Pop threw water onto the burning fence and put the fire out straight away.

"By the way," said Lolli looking puzzled, "how did our garden fence get on fire in the first place?"

Pop looked down at his slippers. "I'm afraid it was my fault, Lolli. I had a bonfire and forgot to see that the flames were put out before we went to bed. A spark must have set fire to the fence!"

"It's out now," smiled Lolli, and there's no harm done."

So before Lolli and Pop went back to bed, they thanked their clever little car and wished him a very goodnight.

A Prince Comes To Visit

In young Mantu's village, deep in the jungle, everyone was getting very excited.

A prince was coming on a very special visit to see the great elephants who lived and worked in the jungle.

"The prince must have heard how big and strong we all are," said the leader of the elephants "and he is going to see for himself!"

"It's a great honour," said Opie the baby elephant to his friend Mantu.

"Yes it is," Mantu replied, "but it will make those elephants more conceited than they already are. If that's possible?"

"Get out of the way you two." the big elephants snapped. "We need to get ready. When the prince comes he will want to meet us. He won't even bother with you!"

So off went the elephants to be dressed up in all their finery.

"I wish I could meet the

prince," said Opie to Mantu.

"So do I" agreed the little boy. "We could both get ready, just in case!" and Mantu climbed up on Opie's back and off they went.

Just before the prince was due to arrive, the biggest elephants marched past looking magnificent.

Opie and Mantu hid in the trees to watch.

"It's just like a parade." whispered Opie wide-eyed.

"They're nothing but a bunch of show-offs!" glowered Mantu.

At last the prince arrived and the whole herd of elephants pressed forward to greet him.

"Help!" cried the prince, stepping back in surprise. "Those huge elephants are making the ground tremble!".........and if the truth were told - the prince was frightened.

"I would like to ride on an elephant," said the prince to his friends, "but these are far too big!"

Then out of the trees stepped Mantu and little Opie.

"Hurrah!" cried the prince, clapping his hands and beaming with joy. "This baby elephant is just the right size for me!" and he climbed up on Opie's back.

You see, no one had told the big elephants that the prince was just a little boy, in fact he was only eight years old!"

Always In A Mess

"I do believe that you attract dirt!" said Ashley's dad as he gazed at him in despair.

Ashley had grass stains all over his clothes. He had mud on his face and hair, and goodness knows what he had over his brand new trainers!

"In exactly one hour from now," went on Ashley's dad, "we are going to meet Grandma at the tea-shop for tea. Get cleaned up as fast as you can - and we'll be off straight away."

"No worries!" grinned Ashley as he messed up all the clean towels.

"I can't possibly get dirty in a tea-shop!"

However, Ashley's dad was not so sure.

Now believe it or not, Ashley hadn't been in the tea-shop five minutes, before the lady who serves the tea, tripped over his foot and spilt a whole tray of cakes...............all over Ashley's dad.

"I'm not in a mess this time. Am I dad?" asked Ashley, still perfectly clean and tidy.

"No, not this time Ashley!" said his dad heaving a big sigh.

Don't Press That Button

Young Mildred Makepeace had a very bad habit - she pressed buttons!

Most of us know which button to press and when to press it.

Unfortunately Mildred did not!

She pressed all the doorbells down the street, then she pressed the button on the fire-alarm - just to see the fire-engine speed past.

"You're a menace!" cried Mildred's mother in despair when her young daughter pressed the wrong button on the washing machine, and the water flooded out all over the kitchen floor.

When people were talking on the telephone, if Mildred walked by, she would press the button and cut the caller off - which was very irritating indeed!

Mildred's mum had lost count of the times she had been stuck in the lift when Mildred pressed the wrong button.

One day in the park, Mildred discovered a button she had never seen before.

"Don't press it Mildred!" yelled her mother.

Without any warning a spurt of ice-cold water hit Mildred in the face and drenched her from top to toe.

Poor Mildred had pressed the button on the drinking water fountain. Strange to say, after that, Mildred never pressed another button.

Sing 'Happy Birthday'

Scott's little cousin April was very quiet and rather shy.

"What a good little girl," people would say. "She never makes a mess, she doesn't make much noise and she's very tidy. In fact she's perfect!"

April was perfect.......until the day that Scott had his birthday party.......

All the young guests were sitting around the table, when in came Scott's mother with his birthday cake. There on top were seven brightly lit candles, just waiting to be blown out.

One, two, three, Scott blew them out in one big breath and everyone sang 'Happy Birthday! Scott's little cousin April sang loudest of all (which surprised everyone - because she was so quiet.)

Now as soon as the children stopped singing and began to get on with the games, April started to scream, (which was very unlike her - because she was so quiet)

Now the only thing that would stop April screaming was the Happy Birthday song.

The guests sang it over and over again. Scott had to sing when the party was over and all through the next day.

Happy Birthday to you! Happy Birthday to you!

While he sang the song, April was happy and quiet, but as soon as he stopped, April would yell and scream.

What was to be done?

Lucky for everyone, Scott's mother went to the toy store and found a little music box - and what do you think it played?

'Happy Birthday to you'

Now Scott's little cousin April is very quiet once more - except when she sings 'Happy Birthday! of course!

Bobbie's Boat

Bobbie the Baker worked hard from morning 'til night.

He had to be at his baker's shop very early indeed.

Bobbie always set his alarm clock to ring at four in the morning. That was the time he started to mix the flour, the water and the yeast, to make the dough, then bake the bread for his customers.

Bobbie loved being a baker and made some of the most delicious bread and tempting cakes you ever tasted.

Although folks came from far and wide to buy his bread, every night when Bobbie closed his shop he always had a few loaves left.

Now Bobbie was a kind-hearted person, and that is why before he went home he filled his baker's basket up with left-over bread, which he fed to the birds who lived on the lake in front of his house.

72

The swans and the ducks and the geese liked the taste of Bobbie's bread, and gobbled it up eagerly.

"I wish we could do something for Bobbie in return!" hissed a large white swan.

"So do we!" cackled the geese as they landed on the water.

Every single evening when Bobbie had returned home and fed the birds, he would get into his tiny boat and row across the lake to visit his girlfriend, who lived on the opposite side of the lake.

But one night when Bobbie stepped into his boat as usual, he got quite a shock - he was standing up to his ankles in icy cold water.

"There's a hole in my boat!" cried Bobbie in dismay, and he just managed to scramble ashore as the boat sank to the bottom of the lake.

"I can't afford to buy another boat," Bobbie told his friends the birds. "I shall never be able to meet my girlfriend again!" and he went inside looking very sad indeed.

So that night the ducks, the geese and the swans held a meeting, and very soon came up with an idea.

Next morning the birds were up and about as early as Bobbie.

"Can you bring your biggest mixing bowl home with you tonight?" asked one of the swans.

"Certainly!" replied Bobbie, who was far too bothered about not seeing his girlfriend to be curious about the bowl.

That night he understood why!

Those clever birds tied long ropes onto the huge mixing bowl and gently towed it across the lake, with Bobbie sitting safely inside.

"At last we can do something for you in return for all the bread you feed us!" chorused the ducks and the geese and the swans.

Seeing The Sights

The zoo-keeper and his wife Norah worked very hard looking after the animals in the zoo.

Sometimes, if every single one of the animals behaved themselves, Norah would think of a special treat that they could all share.

"How would you like to go sightseeing?" Norah asked the animals one day when the zoo was closed.

"Can we visit a big city and see the sights there?" cried the giraffe who usually kept quiet.

"If it's not too far to walk." said the zoo-keeper in a serious voice (although he was winking at Norah.)

"I'll be alright!" the giraffe butted in. "My legs are so long, I'll be there in a jiffy!"

"How about us?" asked hte smaller animals very worried. "We can't walk very far and we don't want to miss our special treat."

Just then a bus drove through the zoo gates and parked in front of the animals.

"This," announced Norah with a wave of her hand, "is a bus especially made for sightseeing"...........all the animals crowded round. "The smallest of you can sit upstairs, the medium size animals can sit downstairs, and the larger animals can sit upstairs and downstairs at the same time!"

It took the animals quite a while to fit into the bus, but at last they were ready for off.

"I think we should go sightseeing more often!" smiled the zoo-keeper.

"I agree!" laughed his wife Norah.

74

Snowdrop Tricks Mr Magic

Mr Magic had a pet rabbit called Snowdrop who helped him with his tricks on stage.

The little white rabbit liked being part of Mr Magic's act, especially when he pulled him out of his top-hat.

"I'm going to play a trick on Mr Magic for a change," giggled Snowdrop, "it will be great fun!"

So he set to work. First he pulled a long string of coloured flags from Mr Magic's pocket, then he plucked a whole pack of cards from behind his ears.

"You'll have to do better than that!" laughed Mr Magic as he produced a bunch of flowers from his sleeve. "I know every trick there is!"

Next day Snowdrop got a letter from his brother, asking if he might come and stay for a while.

"Please tell your brother to come over right away" said Mr Magic kindly. "You never know, he might like to help us in our act."

"I'm sure he'd love that," said Snowdrop with a little secret grin.

When Snowdrop's brother arrived the next day, Mr Magic was already on stage in the middle of his act.

When he came to the very last trick, Mr Magic waved his wand and pulled Snowdrop out of his top-hat as usual.

The audience gasped, then began to clap and cheer...........it wasn't Snowdrop........for there instead was a soft fluffy black rabbit. Poor Mr Magic almost dropped him in surprise.

"That's my brother!" whispered Snowdrop giggling behind the curtain.

"I've tricked you at last!"......and Mr Magic had to agree.

75

Teddy's Invitation

One morning an important envelope arrived for Teddy in the post.

"It isn't my birthday for months," said Teddy puzzled, "although it looks just like a birthday card."

"I can guess what it is!" cried one of the smaller dolls. "It's an invitation. Open it up and tell us who it's from!"

So Teddy did just that. "It's a wedding invitation," gasped Teddy looking shocked, "I've never been to a wedding before."

It was from the bride-doll who was getting married the following Saturday, and she wanted Teddy to come to the wedding.

"Whatever shall I wear?" Teddy asked the other toys. "Does anyone know?"

"You must look very smart," said the soldier-doll. "Try my uniform on for size."

Now when Teddy tried it on, all the toys began to laugh.

"It's a little on the small side," whispered the toy rabbit shyly.

"I think you ought to go down to the costume shop and hire a best suit."

So off went Teddy on the rabbit's advice.

The costume shop was full of very smart clothes. "Better make a start!" said Teddy out loud as he began to try the suits on.

The first one had a coat with tails which made Teddy trip up.

The second was too small. The trousers were too short, the waistcoat was so tight the buttons popped off, and the sleeves of the jacket only reached Teddy's elbows.

"We don't seem to have anything in your size" said the man in the shop as he rolled up his tape-measure.

Sadly Teddy left the shop, but when he reached home he was surprised to see the bride-doll standing in his garden.

"I'm afraid I can't find anything to wear at your wedding!" said Teddy looking glum.

The bride-doll stared at Teddy in surprise. "Just come as yourself. You look just perfect as you are!" and she gave Teddy a kiss and a great big hug.

"How about a top-hat?" the man in the shop asked Teddy. "You should always wear a top-hat at a wedding!"

Teddy tried them all. What a shock he got when he saw himself in the mirror.

The Moon, A Balloon And A Spoon

This is a very strange story about the moon, a balloon and a spoon - but who's to say it isn't true?

It happened late one night when everybody had gone to bed. All the children in the houses had been fast asleep for hours, and all the grown-ups too. Only the cats that sat on the rooftops were wide awake in the moonlight.

Suddenly there came a noise like.......thunder perhaps, or a jet plane maybe, or the roaring, rushing sound of a hurricane........no-one could really say for sure.

All at once everyone was out of bed opening their windows and looking up into the sky.

There it was again, and again, and again. The noise was so loud that it knocked off some of the chimney pots and sent them rolling down the roofs.

"What is it?" the people in the houses cried with fright.

A ginger cat who had been sitting on the roof seemed to know the answer.

"It's the Moon!" he purred, looking very aloof. "The Moon has a bad cold and he keeps on sneezing!" and the ginger cat strolled off to find a quieter rooftop.

Sure enough when the people looked up into the sky, they could see that the Moon had a dreadful cold - red nose and all!

The stars were scattered across the sky, for they found it very difficult to hang on when the Moon was sneezing so hard.

All through that night the Moon sneezed and sneezed. No-one got a wink of sleep and everyone felt very tired and grumpy next morning.

"What are we going to do?" neighbours asked one another - but nobody had the least idea.

"How long does a bad cold usually last?" someone asked the chemist in the shop down the street.

"At least a week," he said gravely, "and in some cases up to a fortnight!"

Everybody groaned. No sleep for a fortnight.........it was unthinkable!.

"What the Moon really needs is a bottle of my best cold medicine," the chemist went on, "that will stop him sneezing in a jiffy."

"This all sounds very silly indeed," said a lady who lived in one of the houses. "How on earth can we give medicine to the Moon?"

"Somebody could float up there in a balloon," said one little boy "they do it all the time in nursery rhymes and fairy stories!"

"That sounds like a very good idea to me," a man spoke up, "I have a hot-air balloon and would gladly help the Moon's bad cold!"

First the medicine had to be mixed. The chemist found everything he needed and put all the ingredients into a great big bowl. He had a giant bottle in his shop window so he carefully poured the cold mixture into that.

"So far so good," smiled the chemist looking very pleased with himself.

"We shall need a giant spoon!" piped up the little boy (whose idea it was in the first place).

"I've just the thing." cried the baker. "I use it to stir my cakes at Christmas time..........I've such a lot to make!" So straight away he ran to his shop to fetch the giant spoon.

The man who owned the hot-air balloon started getting things ready. The little boy (whose idea it was in the first place), was going up in the basket to give the Moon the medicine.

By the time darkness fell and the Moon appeared in he sky, everything was ready.

You could hear that the Moon's cold was no better, in fact he sounded much worse. Even the clouds were being blown all over the place.

80

"Soon we shall be sneezing instead of twinkling." some of the stars grumbled loudly.

At long last the man in the hot-air balloon and the little boy, (whose idea it was in the first place), reached the Moon.

Very, very carefully the little boy gave the Moon the cold medicine from the giant spoon.

"Is it alright to take the whole bottle?" asked the Moon wheezing and sneezing.

"Perfectly alright", the little boy replied, "it says so on the label!"

The cold medicine worked wonders. In next to no time the Moon recovered and all was peace and quiet. Everyone in the houses had a good night's sleep, for there was nothing to disturb their slumbers.......and the cats walked along the rooftops as usual and gazed up at the Moon, who was fast asleep too!

Father Bear Does The Washing Up

Father Bear hated washing up. The cups and saucers weren't too bad, but he simply hated the dirty, greasy pans.

Now in the Bear's house, everyone took turns to wash up, and tonight, was Father Bear's turn.

"What are we having for supper tonight dear?" asked Father Bear from behind his newspaper.

"Omelette with salad," replied Mother Bear. "I'm just going to fetch the pan now!"

"Wonderful," chuckled Father Bear to himself, "that means only one little pan for me to wash up!"

How wrong he was!

Mother Bear had only just begun to cook the omelette, when Baby Bear cried to be lifted out of his high chair................and when Mother returned..........the omelette was burnt and stuck to the pan.

"Oh dear," said Mother Bear, "what a shame, we'll have to have soup instead!"

So she filled a huge pan with thick, tasty soup and left it to simmer on the stove.

Just at that moment there was a telephone call for Mrs Bear, and when she came back................the soup had boiled over.............all down the sides of the pan.

pan, filled it full of boiling water and tossed in the spaghetti.

Suddenly there came a knock at the door. "I'll answer it," cried Father Bear, "while you look after the spaghetti!"

Surprise, surprise, it was the delivery bear with a pile of pizzas!

"Oh dear," said Mother Bear, "I had quite forgotten I'd ordered pizza for supper. What a shame, I needn't have messed up all those pans!"

I think Father Bear will be washing up for quite a while, don't you.

"Oh dear," said Mother Bear, "what a shame, we'll have to have sausages!"

As soon as the sausages were sizzling and spitting in the frying pan, Brenda Bear needed a button stitching on her blouse...........and when Mother Bear returned...........the frying pan was alight and the sausages were burnt to a cinder.

"Oh dear," said Mother Bear, "what a shame, we'll have to have spaghetti!"

So she took down her biggest

Roger's Bow and Arrow

Roger's Gran had a pear tree that grew right alongside the wall of her house.

Sometimes when Roger stayed with his Gran, if the fruit was ready, he would lean out of the bedroom window and pick a juicy, ripe pear.

"Don't forget," said Roger every autumn, "Grans are not supposed to climb ladders, it's far too dangerous. I will pick the pears for you!"

"Very well!" said Gran with a sigh, (because she loved climbing ladders)..... but she said she wouldn't, and Grans always keep their promises!

"Why do the biggest and best pears grow on the end of the branches where no one can reach them?" Gran asked Roger as they were picking the fruit.

"I can't reach them from the ladder or from the bedroom window," said Roger looking puzzled, "but I know how I can!" and he ran indoors.

"What on earth are you going to shoot with that bow and arrow?" Gran gasped. "Not me, I hope!" and she laughed.

Now Roger had tied a string to each of his arrows - which had little suckers in the end instead of sharp tips.

Every time he hit a pear, Roger gave the string a quick tug, and the fruit fell into Gran's outstretched apron.

"Right on target!" cried Roger "Right on!" laughed his Gran.

Colin Thinks Big

Colin Caterpillar and Sylvia Snail were crawling along the garden wall one sunny morning.

"Isn't the world big!" remarked Colin as he gazed around.

"It's huge, it's gigantic, it's enormous, it's vast!" agreed Sylvia, who thought a lot about such things inside that shell of hers.

"It makes me feel so very small," Colin went on.

"But I know a way to change all that!" said Sylvia wisely.

So the two of them spent the rest of that morning collecting the teeniest, weeniest, tiniest things they could find.

Colin collected a crumb, a pea, a shell and a petal. Very soon he had found a feather, a peanut, a button and a berry.

Sylvia brought back a drawing pin, a paper clip, a pen nib, a pin and a needle.

"Look! You're almost a giant Colin!" and off she crawled.

"How small these things are," chuckled Colin, "and look how big I am!"

Mr Wolf's Speed-boat

The three little pigs loved to spend a day by the river just messing about in their small boats.

On fine mornings they would get up early, and if there was no sign of rain, the three pigs would pack a picnic and set off for the river where their boats were moored.

One little pig had a blue and yellow rowing boat, one had a canoe, and the other little pig had a raft made from bits and bobs he'd collected.

Now some times wicked Mr Wolf would creep up behind them At first the three little pigs thought he was after their picnic. But they soon realised that he wanted to eat them, not their food!

But try as he might, Mr Wolf simply couldn't catch the three little pigs, for as soon as they knew he was around, they jumped into their small boats and paddled into the middle of the river where they knew they would be safe.........

......that is until one dreadful day, when wicked Mr Wolf went out and bought a boat of his own.

The three little pigs were paddling their small boats in the middle of the river as usual, when suddenly, out of the reeds zoomed Mr Wolf in a bright red speed-boat!

That bad Mr Wolf raced towards the three little pigs as fast as he could. He sped round and round them churning the water into huge waves. It wasn't long before the small boats were overturned and the three little pigs were tipped into the water.

"Help! Help! Help!" yelled the poor pigs as they bobbed up and down very wet and frightened. But Mr Wolf sped off down the river towards the sea laughing all the way.

As Mr Wolf whizzed through the water, he passed so close to the water-vole's house-boat, that some of the smaller members of the family fell overboard into the river.

This made Mr Wolf laugh even louder. He was having great fun!

Very soon Mr Wolf reached the end of the river. Here were lots of boats going about their business, sailing on the open sea or coming in and out of the harbour.

Without even stopping to think, Mr Wolf drove his speed-boat as fast as he could right through the middle of them. He overturned two yachts and wrecked a motor-boat.

Because of Mr Wolf, a tug almost crashed into a trawler and all the smaller boats had to make for the safety of the harbour.

All of a sudden Mr Wolf's speed-boat stopped. Although he tried with all his might, the wicked wolf could not re-start the engine and his boat began to drift out to sea.

"Help somebody, help!" screamed Mr Wolf "I've stopped! I'm all alone! I can't swim and I'm frightened!"

But nobody heard Mr Wolf. Everyone was far too busy trying to sort out the damage he had caused to the boats in the harbour.

Soon it began to grow dark. No-one remembered Mr Wolf. So he sate alone in his speed-boat until it was dawn, the tide came in and gently washed Mr Wolf back into the harbour.

"I couldn't start my engine!" sobbed Mr Wolf very stiff and cold.

"I'm not surprised," shouted one of the fisherman on board a trawler. "You must have run out of petrol!"

How silly Mr Wolf looked.

When the three pigs heard about his unfortunate adventure, they laughed until they cried.

"Serves him right!" giggled one little pig.

"Lucky we were wearing life-jackets when he overturned our boats!" said another.

"I bet the wicked wolf will never spoil our days out on the river again!".........and the three little pigs went on laughing!

Baby Hedgehog Makes the Dinner

Mrs Hedgehog and her family were all outside working in the garden.

Baby Hedgehog could see how busy they were as he stood by the kitchen door.

Two of the young hedgehogs were digging, two more were hoeing, and the rest were planting vegetable seeds.

"There's such a lot of gardening to be done." said Baby Hedgehog. "Everybody will be very hungry when dinner time comes"...........and as he walked back into the kitchen, he had a wonderful idea. "I shall make the dinner and surprise everybody!"

So straight away Baby Hedgehog took down his mother's cookery book to help him decide what to make for dinner.

Carefully he turned every page. "These recipes all look delicious."

But then Baby Hedgehog remembered that he couldn't read, so he put the cookery book back on the shelf.

'I can make toast and cheese sandwiches," said Baby Hedgehog as he sat at the table, "but they're a bit boring!"

So he jumped down from his stool and looked inside all the kitchen cupboards to see what he could find.

Very soon he came across lots of things that he knew the little hedgehogs liked to eat.

"I shall mix them all together in one big bowl, and then everybody will have a lovely dinner!"

First Baby Hedgehog put in a packet of chocolate biscuits, a tub of vanilla ice-cream and a jug of custard.

Next he found some peaches in a tin "They will do nicely!" said the little hedgehog, very pleased with himself.

"We all love spaghetti with some tomato sauce," so that went into the bowl too.

Then he discovered some jelly beans and half a packet of peanuts.

"They'll do for decoration with a blob of cream on top..........finished at last!"

Baby Hedgehog opened the kitchen drawer, took out a spoon and tried a little sample from the bowl, then he tried a bit more until he began to feel quite sick.

And so it was that at dinner time, when Mrs Hedgehog and all the other little hedgehogs came in feeling very hungry, they found Baby Hedgehog sitting at the table looking rather green.

"I think I'd better make beans on toast for all of us." said Mrs Hedgehog as she looked inside the mixing bowl.

"Nothing for me thank you!" said Baby Hedgehog very quietly.

Tilly's Grin

Baby Tilly was very special. Her Mum and Dad told her so at least twenty times day.

"You're so special!" cooed her Mum.

"My little precious!" smiled her Dad as he tickled Tilly under her chin.

"Let's take her photo!" cried Mum and Dad together.

Now Tilly's photo had been taken every day since she was born,

and on every single one of them she was frowning.

"Give us a grin!" pleaded her Dad.

"Just one little smile!" begged her Mum.

But Tilly just frowned and kept on frowning........until one glorious day........
Tilly woke up and a huge beaming smile spread right across her face. She opened her mouth and gave a great big grin, and there in the middle were two new front teeth!

A String Of Beads

Dolly, Molly and Holly liked to thread beads on a string. They had boxes and jars filled with pretty coloured beads of every shape and size and colour.

Sometimes the girls made necklaces, sometimes they made bracelets, and often they would just thread their beads on a long string.

Dolly, Molly and Holly were always careful to pick up the beads they had dropped on the floor, just in case they got sucked into Mum's vacuum cleaner and were lost for ever.

One day the three girls decided that they would thread the longest string of beads in the world. They set to work and by bedtime had made a necklace that stretched all round the table, and then some!

"Does anyone mind if I borrow this piece of string?" asked Dad as he got up from his chair.

"Be careful!" shrieked all three girls. Too late! Dad pulled the string and hundreds of beads were scattered all over the floor. Dad took one step and went flying too.

So poor Dolly, Molly and Holly had to start threading their beads all over again!